TERRY DEARY'S TALES

TUDORS AND TRAITORS

Illustrated by Helen Flook

A & C BLACK
AN IMPRINT OF BLOOMSBURY
LONDON   NEW DELHI   NEW YORK   SYDNEY

First published by
A & C Black, an imprint of Bloomsbury Publishing plc
50 Bedford Square
London WC1B 3DP

www.bloomsbury.com

ISBN 978-1-4729-0670-0

Printed and Bound by CPI Group (UK) Ltd, Croydon CR0 4YY

1 3 5 7 9 10 8 6 4 2

MIX
Paper from
responsible sources
FSC® C020471

Terry Deary's Tudor Tales

THE PRINCE, THE COOK AND THE CUNNING KING

Illustrated by Helen Flook

A & C BLACK
AN IMPRINT OF BLOOMSBURY
LONDON NEW DELHI NEW YORK SYDNEY

Chapter One
The Cold Kitchen

We stood at the palace door and shivered. The wind was wintry, the grey walls gloomy. I was afraid.

My mother was just about to knock for a second time when the door was tugged open and I found myself looking into the castle kitchen.

A dozen dirty faces stared at me. The servants were sitting round a large table with wooden bowls in front of them.

"Shut the door!" someone moaned.
"It's cold!"

My mother pushed me into the kitchen
and the door slammed behind us with a
boom like the sound of doom.

The dozen pairs of eyes followed us
into the cold kitchen.

There was a huge fireplace with copper pots, iron pans hanging down alongside dead rabbits and geese, and a shrivelled side of bacon. In that fireplace a miserable fire smoked under a small black pot full of pale and pitiful porridge.

A man lifted the pot off the fire and placed it on the table. The servants passed it round and spooned out the watery mess. They ate silently.

The man turned to look at me. He was the fattest man I'd ever seen. Folds of fat almost hid his little, watery eyes and his neck was like a bull's. When he smiled, his teeth were yellow-green and broken. His greasy apron smelled nearly as bad as his breath. He put a hard hand under my chin and tilted my head up. "So, you're the new kitchen maid?"

"This is Eleanor – Ellie," my mother said. "Say hello to Cook, Ellie."

"Hello to Cook, Ellie," I muttered.

The clatter of wooden spoons in the sloppy food stopped. Twelve servants at the table held their breath. Cook's eyes almost vanished in a scowl. Then he grinned.

"A lively lass, eh? Makes a change from this miserable lot!" he said, looking round at the servants who started eating again.

He nodded to my mother. "Leave her with me and I'll take care of her."

My mother left the bundle with my spare clothes and hurried to the door. She opened it and looked back, worried.

"Shut the door!" someone moaned. "It's cold!"

She left me. Alone.

Chapter Two
The Shivering
Servant

The cook looked round the table.
"Lambert Simnel," he hissed.

A boy rose to his feet. He was
as thin as the porridge in
the pot
and
twice as
pale.

"Yes, Cook?" he said, and he shivered.

"Look after young Ellie. Show her where she sleeps. Show her what to do."

"Yes, Cook."

The boy looked back longingly at his half-full bowl of mush. He left the bench and moved towards me, walking almost sideways like a crab. As he passed Cook, the fat man lashed out at Lambert and the boy ducked.

"He didn't do anything!" I cried.

Cook turned his fat face on me. His lips curled back to show those green teeth.

"Lambert has been a wicked, wicked boy, haven't you, Lambert?"

"Yes, Cook."

"He doesn't deserve a smack on the head!" I said, and my face was hot in that cold kitchen.

"No," Cook said softly. Then a dirty finger prodded me in the shoulder and he exploded with stinking breath in my face, "He deserves an axe on the back of his scrawny neck."

Suddenly, he picked up a meat-axe from a table and shook it wildly. "He deserves to be executed. Don't you, Lambert?"

"Yes, Cook," the miserable boy murmured.

"Now take her to the room over the stables and show her where she'll be sleeping."

Lambert nodded, gave me a quivering smile, picked up my bundle and nodded for me to follow him. I stopped at the door and looked back to see one of the servants emptying Lambert's porridge bowl.

Chapter Three
The Scratching
Straw

"I have to sleep *here*?" I asked Lambert.
  He nodded and dropped
my bundle on to
a pile of straw
in the
loft.

"Sleep on the straw," he said. "Use the blanket to cover you. It's warm with the horses below you in the stable."

I was staring at my bed.

"The straw moved," I whispered.

Lambert laughed. "That'll just be a rat. I have a special friend rat," he said.

Suddenly he darted to the top of the stairs and looked down. "People listen at doors here, you know?"

He scuttled back to me. "I call my rat Henry. After the King!"

"The King would be furious, if he knew," I said.

"The King is the biggest rat of all," he said wildly. "Why do you think everyone in the palace is so miserable? Because the King is so mean. We eat the cheapest food.

Even his wife, Queen Elizabeth, is made
to patch her dresses. She has tin buckles
on her shoes when a queen should
have silver!"

I sat down on the straw. "Cook looks
fat enough," I said.

Lambert dashed to the top of the steps
and back again. "He steals the King's food.
If we did it we'd be whipped. But Cook
has the key to the pantry."

"Why did Cook call you 'wicked'?" I asked.

Lambert ran to the top of the stairs and back for the third time. He spoke quickly.

"King Henry stole the crown of England. The real king should be Prince Edward, but he was locked in the Tower of London by King Henry Tudor."

"I've heard the story. He's still locked away there, isn't he?"

Lambert shook his head so hard I thought it would fall off on to the rat-filled straw. "Edward escaped!" he squeaked.

"How do you know, Lambert?" I asked quietly.

"Because it's me! I'm Edward, Earl of Warwick. I'm the real king of England!"

Chapter Four
The Midnight Meeting

That day, I learned my duty as kitchen maid.

I scrubbed pans with sand and I swept the floor. I made bread till my arms ached and I carried buckets of water till my shoulders were numb.

We had bread and cheese for lunch – but Cook didn't eat with us. He disappeared into the pantry for two hours and came out with food dribbling down his chin, looking sleepy. Then it was time to make the evening meal for the King and his court.

Cook breathed over me. "If yo
hard, one day you may become a se
maid and get to see the King."

One day.

I saw him sooner than that. I sank
into my straw that night as the clocks
struck eleven.

I dozed a little. I heard the bells chime
midnight.

That was when guards came for me.
They came quietly with a horn lantern
that barely lit the bat-black night.

One of the men,
the tall one, pressed a hand
over my mouth as a sign that I should
make no sound.

The horses stirred in
the stable below as
I groped my
way down
the stairs
into the
freezing
courtyard.

We entered the kitchen into air that
was thick with stale food and smoky
smells. The guard
opened the lantern
and led me up
the stairs.

I was so tired I could hardly drag myself on. At last we came to the massive doors that led into the great hall.

The room was warmed by a log fire and that lit the room, too. The high, carved thrones were empty. But a man in a dressing gown sat in front of the fire and smiled a thin-lipped smile into the flames.

The tall guard spoke for the first time. "Your Grace? We've brought you the girl."

The man turned and waved a hand for the guards to leave. He grinned at me. His teeth were a little black with rot. It wasn't a pleasant smile. "Come in, Eleanor, and warm yourself."

I dropped a low curtsey to Henry Tudor, King Henry VII of England. "Thank you, Your Grace," I said humbly.

He gave a short laugh. "Eleanor, my dearest niece. You must call me Uncle Henry!"

Chapter Five
The Crafty King

"How was your work in the kitchen?"
King Henry asked.

"It nearly killed me, Uncle," I groaned.

I stretched and yawned wearily as I sat
on a bench at the fireplace.

He nodded. "But no one suspects you?
They all believe you're just a common
serving girl?"

"Yes, Uncle, we've fooled them," I said.
"No one could guess I'm Lady Eleanor
Tudor of Pembroke in Wales."

"Good," he said, rubbing his hands in front of the fire. "Then you are the perfect spy. We Tudors must stick together. I can trust no one outside of my family. There are thousands who want me dead, you know. Dead as a duck's toenail!"

The King stroked the fur collar on his gown and the collar moved. It was a small brown monkey. It looked at me, then went back to sleep.

"There are rebels and traitors everywhere."

"Yes, Uncle, I know," I said.

Mother had told me of the danger. If Henry Tudor lost the throne, then our family back in Wales would suffer, too. They might even kill us the way they killed the Princes in the Tower.

"Have you met Lambert 'Simple' Simnel?"

"Yes, Uncle."

"Did your mother tell you about him?"

"Yes, Uncle. Lambert says he's Prince Edward, but really he's an organ-maker's son from Oxford," I said. "The real Prince Edward is still locked in the Tower of London."

The King stroked his long chin. "He may look a little bit like Prince Edward.

The trouble is, my enemies put a crown on Lambert's head and sent an army from Ireland to kill me!"

"But you won the battle and captured Lambert. You made him a kitchen boy to show what a good, kind king you are," I said.

"I did! There are still people who think Simple Simnel could take my throne. There's only one person who knows for sure who that boy in the kitchen really is ... and that's the boy in the kitchen!"

My Uncle was quivering with so much rage the monkey on his shoulder stirred.

"Now he's afraid so he says he's not Edward. First he is – then he isn't. What's the truth?"

"I'll find out for you, Uncle," I promised. "What will you do if he is the true king?"

Uncle Henry blinked in surprise. "Why, have him killed, of course!"

Chapter Six
The Cruel
Cook

I worked in the kitchen
till my fingers bled
and my nails cracked.

My fair skin was
roasted when I
turned the meat over
the fire and my bare

feet were black
with dirt.

When I got
home to Wales I'd
make sure servants
had a better life
than this.

On the fourth day I struggled to carry a leather bucket of water from the well in the yard.

Fat Cook told me to hurry and swung his boot at my backside. I stumbled and spilled the water.

"Stupid girl," he snarled. "You'll have to do it all over again!"

I sighed, picked up the empty bucket and trudged back to the well. Lambert helped me carry it back to the door.

"He's a bully," Lambert said.

"Then I'll have to teach him a lesson," I snapped.

Lambert stopped and looked at me carefully. "You're a kitchen maid – what can you do?"

I almost blurted, "The King is my uncle and I can have Cook executed with his own meat-axe!" but I had to keep my secret. I still had to fool Lambert into telling me the truth. I said, "There is some yellow-dock plant in the pantry, isn't there?"

Lambert nodded.

"Can we get some?"

"It's locked by Cook," he said, "but I can open locked doors."

I grinned. "How did you learn that?"

"My father made organs in Oxford and I helped with the locks on the lid. I know all about them."

I stopped in the freezing yard. "I thought your father was the Duke of Clarence and you were the true king?"

Lambert laughed. "That's right. But I was switched when I was a baby to save me from being done away with. The organ-maker's son was brought up as Edward ... and I was brought up as the organ-maker's son! I still think of him as my father. The rebels knew that – but they died in battle."

"But does Unc– er ... King Henry know that?"

"No! If he did he'd execute me. I'm a bit simple – but I'm not mad. Of course, no one knows the truth," he laughed.

"Except me," I said.

"Except you – and you're not going to tell the King, are you?"

Chapter Seven
Ellie's Revenge

The kitchen was quiet. The servants watched us, open-mouthed.

Cook had locked himself in the pantry for lunch. I put my ear to the door and heard him snore. I stood aside and let Lambert work on the lock with a knife. In a few moments it clicked open.

The leather hinge creaked. I peered round the door. Cook snored on. His wine sat on the bench beside him.

The pantry was full of cooked meats and pastries, cheeses and bread, wine, honey and herbs. It was like a treasure chest. I passed a large cheese out to the servants and they hurried to a corner to carve it and eat it before Cook woke up.

The stone jar of yellow-dock leaves
scraped as I lifted it from the shelf. Cook
stirred. He snorted. He belched. He
smiled in his sleep.

I rubbed the leaves between my hands
and let the powder fall
into his wine cup.

Lambert gasped. "But ..."
"Shhhh!"
I put more powder in the cup.
"But he'll ..."
"Shhhh!"

I put the empty jar back on the shelf. We crept out and Lambert locked the door.

We waited.

An hour later, Cook came out, red-faced and shouting orders. We scuttled around the kitchen like the rats in my hayloft, making dinner for the royal family and their guests.

King Henry was mean with his money, but he always put on a good feast when he had guests. We baked a fish pie, roasted pheasants and a baby pig, boiled dishes of peas and made cups of rose-flavoured custard. Six o'clock chimed. Dinner was ready to serve.

Cook clutched his fat gut – that was the yellow-dock powder starting to work.

Lambert chewed a knuckle nervously. "Yellow-dock makes you run to the jakes," he whimpered.

"Yes, Cook will need the toilet very soon – and for a long time," I said. "That's my revenge for him kicking me."

Cook rubbed his gut and tried to smile.

"A feast fit for a king!" he cried. "I will lead the way," he told the serving men. "King Henry can tell me to my face how great I am!" He turned on us. "You stay here and start clearing up or I'll whip you raw!"

But when he left we followed the procession to the great hall.

Chapter Eight
Greedy Guts

Lambert and I looked through a crack in the door. Uncle Henry sat at the top table with his guests from France. Their rich robes of crimson and gold, peacock blue and leaf green, were as fine as the ones I'd left at home.

And now I had Lambert's secret I could set off for Wales very soon. But first there was the business of Cook to finish.

"My Lords!" Cook cried.

Silence fell on the great hall. Suddenly the smile slid from his face like jelly off a plate. He clutched his gut and let out the loudest and most disgusting sound I have ever heard.

Pfffffththththththth-tttttttt...

"Sorry, Your Grace!" he groaned and repeated the sound.

Pffffththththththththth-ttttttttt...

"Oh, I need the jakes!" he cried and rushed to the door at the side of the hall.

"Not there!" Uncle Henry called.

Too late. Cook tore open the toilet door.

The Queen, who was in the jakes at the time, screamed, "Help, guards! Help!"

The guards drew their swords and rushed to grab Cook. He barged past them and ran for the main door where we were hiding.

"Don't arrest me yet!" he wailed as he rushed past us, smelling like a drain and his guts gurgling like one, too.

"I need the jakes!"

Cook was fat but ran like a greyhound.

The guards ran faster. They caught him when he reached the door to the jakes in the west tower.

"Please! Please! Please ... *Pffffthththththt-tttttttt* ... just let me go to the ... *Pffffthth-ththth-tttttttt* ... jakes."

The guards grabbed him and dragged him towards the dungeon.

"Oh, no-o-o-o-o!" Cook sobbed. "Now look what you've made me do-o-o-o-o!"

It was the last I saw of him. Of course, I wasn't around for much longer. Cook would be sacked when he was finally released. I stayed long enough to see how happy Lambert and the servants were with their new cook. Long enough to say goodbye to Lambert Simnel – 'traitor'.

"Now that Cook's gone I'm really happy, Ellie," he said.

"As happy as a prince?" I asked.

"Happier," he laughed.

I never told him I was a Tudor – his deadliest enemy.

That evening I went to my hayloft and packed my bundle of clothes.

All I wanted was a warm bath, my own bed and my Welsh home. But before I left I had to tell Uncle Henry the truth about Lambert Simnel.

Chapter Nine
The Terrible
Truth

The guards came for me as midnight chimed.

"Well, Eleanor? Have you learned the truth?" my uncle asked me as he sat before the fire. The monkey turned its head as if waiting for my answer.

"I have," I said.

"Is the boy Lambert Simnel or is he Prince Edward?" he asked.

"Is your executioner's axe sharp?"
I asked.

Uncle licked his thin lips. "It is."

I smiled. "A pity. He won't be needing it. Lambert Simnel is ... Lambert Simnel. The man he calls father is an Oxford organ-maker."

Well? I was telling the truth, wasn't I?

"He's a harmless boy," I said.

"Thank you, Eleanor. The boy can live. The world can see we Tudors are firm, but fair," he said.

I thought of Cook in the dungeon. "Yes, Uncle Henry. The world can see it doesn't pay to tangle with a Tudor."

Afterword
Lambert's Story

The Prince, the Cook and the Cunning King is a story based on real people and events in Tudor times.

Edward, Earl of Warwick, had more right to be king of England than Henry Tudor. So Henry Tudor locked him in the Tower of London, then had himself crowned Henry VII.

Henry's enemies found eleven-year-old Lambert Simnel in Oxford and thought he looked a lot like the imprisoned prince. They taught him to act like Prince

Edward, then they took him to
Ireland where they raised an army.
They planned to invade England, beat
Henry in battle and put Lambert on
the throne – though of course, they
would really run the country for him.

But, when they met Henry's army
at the Battle of Stoke Field, they were
beaten. Lambert was taken prisoner
and Henry sent him to work in his
castle kitchens.

The real Prince Edward stayed in
the Tower of London. Twelve years
later, there was a plot to free Prince
Edward from the Tower. King Henry
did not want to take any chances.
He had the real Edward executed.

Lambert Simnel became a loyal
servant and was released from

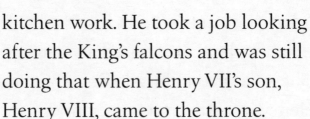

kitchen work. He took a job looking after the King's falcons and was still doing that when Henry VII's son, Henry VIII, came to the throne.

There is just a chance that Edward and Lambert were switched as babies. (Many people in England believed that at the time.) If Lambert knew that then, as in the story, he kept quiet. Sensible. After all ... it doesn't pay to tangle with a Tudor!

THE THIEF, THE FOOL AND THE BIG FAT KING

Illustrated by Helen Flook

A & C BLACK
AN IMPRINT OF BLOOMSBURY
LONDON NEW DELHI NEW YORK SYDNEY

Chapter One
Cowards and
Coffins

"Lay-deez and gennle-men!" my father
cried to the crowd that gathered round.
"See this poor, hungry little boy?" he
roared, pointing at me.

People drifted from every corner of the churchyard to see what was going on. There must have been five hundred people in St Paul's churchyard that day: meeting friends, doing business or just watching the entertainers. Entertainers like me and my father. He kicked me on the ankle.

"Oh!" I cried. "Oh! Oh! Oh! I am so-o-o hungry! I would do anything for a crust of bread!"

The truth was, I was full of mutton pie, but you have to put on an act if you want to make some money.

About fifty people pushed and jostled to get a better view. My father lifted me onto the rough wooden coffin we had brought with us.

"This little boy is so-o-o hungry he is willing to risk his life to make a few pennies."

"What's he going to do?" a
tangle-haired girl called out. "Jump off
the coffin?"

The crowd laughed. Father turned red.

"He is going to let me stab him!" my
father shouted, and the laughter died
suddenly.

"Tshah!" the girl sneered. "I'll give you
a penny if you let me do it." She pulled
a knife from the pocket of her scruffy
brown dress and waved it under my nose.
"I'll cut his head clean off."

My father tried to ignore her. He pulled

off his green cap and held it out. "Come on, lay-deez and gennle-men. Give just a few pennies to see this terrible sight!"

"Oh!" I cried. "Oh! Oh! Oh! I am so-o-o hungry! I would do anything for a crust of bread!"

A thin man in a yellow jerkin and red trousers shouted, "Let's see you stab him first!"

The rest of the crowd agreed. "Stab him first!"

And the tangle-haired girl said, "Let
me do it!"

My father slapped his cap back on.
"Oh, very well," he snapped. "I will stab
him." He turned to me. "Are you ready,
my dear, darling little boy?"

I squeezed my eyes tight shut and
squeaked, "Yes, my dear father. But if
I die, please give my love to Mummy!"

The crowd shuffled and sniffed
and looked unsure now.

Even the tangle-haired girl in the scruffy dress was watching in silence.

"If I get it wrong and I kill you, will you forgive me, little James?"

"I forgive you, Father," I sighed.

I wished he'd get on with it. But I knew he was waiting till everyone in the graveyard was watching. The bigger the audience, the more money we'd make.

"Lay-deez and gennle-men," Father
went on and I opened my eyes a little.
"This is no trick. See this knife – it is
sharp enough to shave a swine!"

He reached forward, grabbed the girl in
the brown dress and sliced off a lump of
her tangled hair with a stroke.

The crowd gasped.

"Oi! What are you doing?" the girl raged and her face, under the dirty smudges, glowed red with anger. I tried not to laugh.

My father turned to me. He raised the knife high in the air so the spring sunlight glittered on the blade. It was so quiet, I'll swear you could hear the worms below the graveyard chewing away at the bodies.

The knife swept down and struck me in the stomach.

Chapter Two
Blood and
Bladders

"Oh, Father!" I gasped and clutched at my stomach. The cold blood trickled through my fingers. The crowd shouted and cried in confusion. "Oh, dear Father, I think you have killed me!"

I moved to the end of the coffin and fell into his arms.

"My son, my James, my little Jimmy!" he wept. "I have your coffin here," he said.

I let myself go limp in his arms.

He kicked open the lid and lowered me into the box.

The lid slammed and I was in darkness.

That didn't matter. I'd done this fifty times before, all over England and Wales. I didn't need light. I wriggled out of the blood-wet shirt and untied the pig's stomach that was strapped to my waist.

There was still some pig's blood in it and I wrapped it quickly in the shirt and stuffed it in the hidden cubbyhole at the head of the coffin.

I took off the wooden board that was strapped to my belly – the one that had stopped the knife from really going into me.

I placed it, clean side out, over the secret cubbyhole so the blood-stained shirt was hidden. The board fitted perfectly – it was made to. No one who looked at the

coffin would find the shirt. I groped at my feet and found a clean shirt and struggled into it. I could hear muffled voices through the thin wood. Father was crying, "Is there no one who can help me in my hour of despair? I cannot even afford to bury my little James!"

Then I heard a woman's voice say,
"I have heard of a spell that will raise
the dead – if you say it quickly enough.
And it will only work the once!"

I heard the crowd gasp and shuffle
away. I heard them mutter "Witchcraft!"
in terror, and you could be hanged for
witchcraft.

"Please say the words, good woman!"
Father groaned.

"Sorry, dear sir," she sighed. "I need
silver and gold in my hands or the spell
will never work – and I am a poor
woman!"

"Has no one any silver or gold?"
Father cried.

There was a chinking and tinkling
as the crowd opened their purses and
placed the money in the woman's hands.

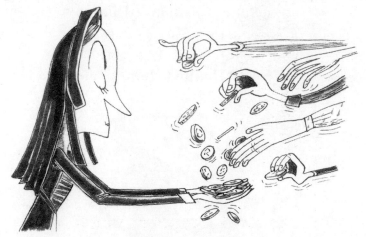

I heard the woman place her hands on
the top of the coffin.

I heard her rest her head on top of the coffin lid...

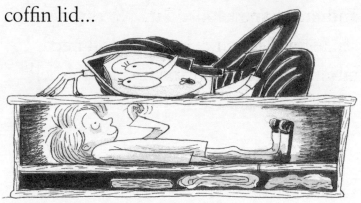

...and mutter the strange Egyptian words she had learned.

Ofano, Oblamo, Ospergo.
Pax Sax Sarax.
Afa Afca Nostra.
Cerum Heaium Lada Frium!

Then the coffin lid was thrown open and the woman looked in. No one could see me as I gave her a quick grin and mouthed, "Hello, Mum!"

Chapter Three
Cutpurses and Confusion

My mother called, "Rise from your coffin, child."

I blinked and sat up.

I struggled to my feet and felt my
stomach. The crowd gasped. They'd seen
the blood flow and they'd seen it stain my
shirt. Now my shirt was as white as the
April clouds above the churchyard.

Father fell to his knees and kissed
Mother's hands. "Thank you, good lady –
a father's thousand thanks!"

The crowd sighed, "Ahhhh!" and this time, as Father passed round the hat, it was filled.

But no one noticed the girl with the hair as wild as a bramble bush.

"Here!" she screeched. "It was all a trick! Here's the shirt and here's a pig's bladder full of blood. You've been robbed!"

She must have slipped round to the open coffin and opened the secret panel. Now she was holding up the blood-soaked shirt.

Suddenly, an angry mob snatched at Father's hat. He was smacked with the blade of a gentleman's sword and I was kicked with a dusty boot. We went to pick up the coffin, but the crowd had already trampled it to firewood.

Then there was a new cry in the crowd.

"My purse has gone! There are cutpurses in the churchyard!"

The mob forgot about us as more people discovered they had lost their purses of silver.

We took the chance to escape from St Paul's, hurry down Fleet Street and hide in the stinking darkness of The Dead Duck tavern.

Mother flopped on to a bench and sighed. "That cutpurse saved us a lot of trouble!"

Father shook his head angrily. "No, the cutpurse *caused* us all the trouble! It was that girl in the brown dress. She showed the crowd how we did the swindle.

"She *knew* there would be trouble. It's an old cutpurse trick. While people are in a riot, they forget about the purses that are hung from their belts. She ran around and stole their cash."

I nodded sadly. "She had the knife all ready, didn't she?"

Father groaned. "We've no money."

"No coffin," Mother added.

"No blood bladder," I reminded them.

"And no bed for the night," the fat landlord said softly. "You already owe me for the mutton pies you had at breakfast. If you've no money, you can get out now!"

We rose wearily to our sore feet and trudged to the door.

"Things can't get much worse," Father said.

Oh, but they could!

Chapter Four
A Fool and a Father

A man stepped out from the shadow of a doorway. He wore a yellow jerkin and red trousers; he was the man from the churchyard.

He placed a hand on my father's shoulder and Father drew his dagger fast as a butterfly's wing. "What do you want? Money? We haven't any. Not a penny! Go rob someone else," Father hissed.

But the man stood in father's way still.

"Are you a fool?" my mother asked him.

"Yes," the man replied.

"What?" I gasped.

"Yes."

"Yes, what?"

"Yes, I'm a fool."

"You don't look stupid," Mother said.

"No, I mean I'm a fool at the court of King Henry VIII. I am Will Somers, the king's jester," he told us eagerly.

"Are you serious?" Father asked.

"No, I'm fool-ish!" the man giggled. We didn't laugh.

"I entertain the king with jests and songs and dancing and juggling."

He leapt into the air...

...spun round, landed on a pile of horse droppings and slipped on his backside.

This time we laughed.

The fool didn't. He picked himself up.

"Your act in St Paul's churchyard would be perfect for the king. He loves disgusting things like that. Will you come to Hampton Court Palace with me? I have a carriage in the tavern courtyard all ready."

"Will we be paid?" Father asked.

"With a purse of gold if the king likes you," Will Somers said.

"Our coffin will need to be replaced," Father added.

"Of course."

"Then show us to the carriage," Father grinned and slapped an arm round the skinny man's yellow jerkin.

And that's how a family of fairground cheats came to perform before King Henry VIII of England...

Chapter Five
A Fat King and Some Cards

King Henry was as fat as a hog. His red face had six chins, and greedy little eyes glinted with the torchlight and golden chains around his neck.

His sly-eyed queen,
Anne Boleyn,
watched us
with a sneer.

Henry's
pasty-faced
daughter, Mary,
trembled and prayed.
Father put on his grandest voice that
night. Every time he spoke he said,
"Your Majesties, my lords, ladies and
gentlemen..."

I thought he was never going to stab me! But at last the knife swept down.

I gasped, I staggered, I wailed, I fell. Princess Mary cried out.

My hands shook so much I fumbled with the boards and just got it in place before my mother threw the coffin lid open.

The king roared and clapped. The rich

lords sat in their velvet gowns of scarlet and gold, cornflower blue and marigold orange, and colours from every rainbow that had ever shone. When they saw Henry had enjoyed the show, they joined in with polite clapping.

Anne Boleyn still sneered.

Will Somers looked pleased as he showed us down to the kitchens to eat.

A heavy purse jangled on Father's broad belt. Life was good.

"Can you play cards?" Will Somers asked.

Father looked at Mother sharply. "A little," he said.

"Father can make a fortune cheating at cards in the taverns," I was going to say, but Mother stepped heavily on my

foot so I said, "Father can make a for ...
ouch, my foot ... sorry, Mother ... ooooh!
My toes are crushed like a squatted fly!"

Will Somers said, "The king enjoys
a game of mumchance. Do you play
mumchance?"

Father acted as if he didn't know.
"Er ... we all name a card. Then we turn
the cards one at a time. The first one to
see their own card wins, is that right?"

"That's right," came a rumbling, rich voice from the doorway. We turned to see the king limp into the kitchens.

His fat legs were covered in bandages. They say he had sores on his legs that wouldn't heal. Blood had begun to seep through the bandages and the smell was worse than The Dead Duck's mutton pies.

We bowed. The king sat heavily at a kitchen table and gave a huge belch.

As Will Somers rushed to hand the king a flagon of wine, the king ordered, "Sit down, you rogues. Give me a chance to win back some of that gold you earned tonight."

Father sat down happily. He always won. Always.

But by the time the clock chimed midnight, Father had lost every last gold piece.

Chapter Six
Cheats Beats

It happened like this. Father could remember every card in the pack. He knew what cards were coming next and he named one to make sure he always won. Half-past eleven chimed...

...and our pile of gold was growing huge.

Quarter to twelve chimed… The gold was yellow, but Henry's fat face was purple with rage.

Will Somers looked on and his face was white with fear. He served Henry more wine and brought a cup for Mother and Father.

As he served Father, he whispered, "If you want to keep your head, let the king win! He hates losing!"

Father swallowed hard and scowled. Father won the next game.

Henry was down to his last two pieces of gold. He put them in the middle of the table.

"Three of hearts," Henry growled.

"Five of spades," Father said quietly.

Mother turned the cards. The three of diamonds stared up at us.

"Three of hearts!" Henry cried and swept the cards off the table. He passed them back to Mother.

"It was the three of diamonds," Father said.

Henry's bloated face grew still larger. He spoke slowly. "Do you know what happens to a man who calls his king a liar?"

Father shook his head.

"He is taken to the Tower of London and tortured until he says he is sorry. And when he's said he is sorry he is taken to Tower Hill and hanged," Henry explained. "That was the three of hearts. What was it?"

Father set his jaw hard.

Before he could speak, Mother cut in, "It was the three of hearts."

Father glared at her but stayed quiet as Henry pushed the four gold pieces back into the middle of the table.

"Again!" he ordered.

We played on. Henry cheated, Henry laughed. Henry won back all his money. He also took all the money we had earned that night.

Midnight chimed. Henry gathered the gold and staggered to his feet.

"Goodnight, Master Magician," he snorted. "It seems your magic let you down. Now get out of my palace, you are making it stink."

So we found ourselves on the dark road outside the palace with a long walk back to the city and not a penny in our pockets. Except...

Chapter Seven
The Thief in the Shadows

When I saw the way the game was going,
I had walked over to Father's side and
rested a hand on
the table beside
the gold he
had left.

I wrapped
a fist around
one gold
piece and
sat back to
watch. Father lost
everything – but
I held onto that one gold piece.

When the sun began to rise, we were back in the city. Our feet were aching after the fifteen-mile walk. And we were starving.

"No money for food or shelter," Father groaned.

That was when I pulled out the gold piece from my pocket. He snatched it from me without a word of thanks and stalked off to The Dead Duck.

I stepped into the gloom. After the bright morning light I could hardly see. But I saw the shadow of a shadow in the far corner.

Something moved towards the back door. As the door opened, light spilled in and I could see her clearly. It was the girl in the brown dress. The cutpurse.

She'd seen us enter and she was running away.

I raced across the bar-room, pushed tables and benches aside and spilled ale mugs.

I was into the stable yard at the back and saw her diving under the belly of a horse. The horseshoes sparked off the cobbles as the horse stamped and almost struck me as I dived after the girl.

As she scrambled to her feet, I was there before her. I grabbed at the bag on her shoulder and it tore – spilling the purses full of coins on to the cobbles.

She looked at me, as poisonous as
Henry VIII's leg.

I held tight to the remains of the bag
and a couple of purses. "If I go to the
constable with these, you'll hang."

She shrugged. "You don't know my
name or where I live. The constable
would never find me."

At that moment, the back door of
the tavern opened and the fat landlord
looked out, as greasy as his apron.

"What's happening, Meg?" he asked.

The girl groaned. "Shut up, Dad!"
Then she groaned again.

I nodded. "So, you're called Meg and
you live at The Dead Duck."

She drew her knife – the one she used
for cutting purses. "What are you going
to do?" she asked.

Chapter Eight
The Cutpurse
and the Coffin

I grinned. "Make a deal with you," I said.

Inside The Dead Duck we all sat around the table. Me and my family, Meg and her dad. The two men shook hands.

"It's a fine idea," the landlord said.

My father nodded. "We take our show on the road again. But this time, Meg calls us "cheats" and starts a riot. While the mob is crowding round us, Meg nips their purses. We meet up later and share the money."

We shared the money from Meg's purses and it was enough to buy us a horse and cart.

A week later we were on the road and travelling all around Britain. It was a hard

and dangerous life we lived for the next
five years. But it kept us going through
the hard days of Henry VIII's reign. In
time, we made enough money to buy a
tavern and give up our lives of trickery
and theft ... although Father still makes
some money from mumchance games.

Now some people may say that what
we did was not honest. It was cheating.

When we were caught, we were put in
the stocks and
whipped.

If Meg had been caught, she could have been hanged.

When fat King Henry VIII cheated, he got away with it because he was king.

When Father stabbed me, it was a game and no one was hurt.

When Henry sent sly-eyed Anne Boleyn and his fifth queen, little Catherine Howard, to be beheaded, it was for real.

So who was the biggest cheat?

Even Will Somers knows the answer to that ... and he's a fool!

Afterword
The Terrible
Truth

*The Thief, the Fool and the Big Fat
King* is a story based on real people
and events.

In Tudor times, St Paul's
churchyard in the centre of London
was a meeting place for all sorts of
people. Even in the church itself,
traders bought and sold stuff. There
were shows in the churchyard and
some of them were tricks – made
to fool people into giving money.
The pig's bladder trick worked well,

though one day a drunken "victim" forgot to put a wooden board under his shirt and was really stabbed to death.

King Henry VIII took the throne when his father died and was one of the richest kings in the world. But he wasted his careful father's wealth. His court fool was Will Somers and we know a little about Will because several books were written about him.

By the time Henry married Anne Boleyn, he didn't have a lot of money to waste on card games. He'd spent it all. Henry loved to play – but hated to lose.

Henry VIII was like a big spoilt child – he had to have his own way. When he didn't get it, he turned

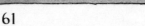

violent and two of his wives were beheaded because of his vicious temper.

Henry VIII was not the sort of man you'd want to play cards with – or, if you did, you'd be happy to lose your money to save your life!

TERRY DEARY'S TUDOR TALES

THE MAID, THE WITCH AND THE CRUEL QUEEN

Illustrated by Helen Flook

A & C BLACK
AN IMPRINT OF BLOOMSBURY
LONDON NEW DELHI NEW YORK SYDNEY

Chapter One
The Messenger in Gold and Red

I remember the day Queen Mary Tudor came to our town. It was the most fearsome, exciting and heart-stopping day of my life. I'll remember it if I live to be a hundred.

I was a serving girl at Lord Scuggate's manor house – a small castle, really. And I was invisible!

No, really!

I carried the food and the wine from the kitchen to the table and all the grand folk in the great hall ignored me.

They never said "Please", they just held out a wine cup to be filled. They never, ever said "Thanks!". It was as if I wasn't there. Invisible in my shabby black dress.

My mouth stayed shut. But my eyes could see and my ears could hear. That summer evening there was a sudden hammering on the door. Lord Scuggate looked furious.

"Who dares to knock at a Scuggate door that way?" he demanded.

I hurried over the rushes on the stone floor and opened the door. A young man in a coat of blood-red and gold threw his handsome head up and marched in. The hounds by the fireside growled.

"Lord Scuggate of Bewcastle?" the young man asked, and his voice whined like a leaking trumpet.

"Who wants to know?" his lordship asked. "What sort of slabberdegullion are you to come barging in on Lord Scuggate and his guests?"

Sir James Marley of Roughsike squeaked and tried to shake Lord Scuggate's arm.

His lordship shook him off.

"I'll have you stripped and whipped and dragged at the cart's tail all the way to the gallows!" he yelled at the messenger.

He swelled like a pig's bladder that the boys blow up to play football. His face was purple. "I'll have you..."

"No, your lordship!" Sir James squawked. "Look at the badge on his coat."

"Shut up, man," Lord Scuggate snapped without taking his eyes off the messenger. "I'll have you hanged by the neck and I don't care who your master is..."

"Mistress," the shocked messenger mumbled.

"Who your mistress is!" Lord Scuggate snorted. "I see by your badge you wear the sign of..."

He stopped. Everyone was looking at the floor. Even the dogs that chewed their bones stopped crunching.

The only sound was Lord Scuggate spluttering as if someone had stuck a needle in his pig-bladder face. "...the sign of ... er ... the sign of..."

"Her Majesty Queen Mary Tudor of England," the messenger said quietly. Lord Scuggate grinned weakly showing his broken and yellow teeth. "And you are very, very welcome to Bewcastle Hall, my dear young friend!"

Chapter Two
The Cruel
Killing Queen

The messenger had said that the queen
would be passing through Bewcastle on
a tour of the Scottish Borders. She would
stop at Scuggate
Hall for
lunch the
next
day.

When the young man in red and gold
had gone, the Bewcastle men muttered
over their wine cups as the invisible maid
heard their terrible talk.

"Down in London, they call the queen 'Bloody Mary' because she burns anyone who doesn't worship at a Catholic church," Sir James Marley of Roughsike said quietly.

"She'd burn us if she found anyone who doesn't go to church," Father Walton of Catlowdy Church warned them.

Lord Scuggate looked at him sharply. "It's your job to make sure people go to church," he said.

The priest in the velvet cloak spread his hands and smirked. "My lord, it is you the queen will blame, and you the queen will burn."

Lord Scuggate's blotched face turned pale. "Everyone in Bewcastle goes to church... Well ... they go at Easter and Christmas anyway, don't they?"

The men brought their heads closer together.

"We could get all the Bewcastle folk together and have a march through the town to the church, just as Queen Mary arrives," Father Walton said.

"All carrying crosses," Sir James Marley added.

"And singing hymns," Lord Scuggate put in. "The queen will love that!"

"Would the town people do it?" Father Walton asked, and his bald head shone yellow in the light of the torches.

"They will if we promise them a few barrels of beer!" Lord Scuggate chuckled.

The men laughed, and held out their wine cups for me to fill.

"Old Nan doesn't drink," Father Walton said.

Lord Scuggate sighed.

"Who's Old Nan?" Sir James asked as he cleaned his fingernails with his knife.

"A wise woman who lives out at Butterburn in the hills," Lord Scuggate snapped. "Some say she is a witch. But the

truth is she just mixes herbs and cures
made from the plants on the moors. I use
them myself," he said. "But
you wouldn't get her into
a church or singing
hymns."

"Perfect!" Sir James cried and waved
his knife. "Queen Mary likes to see her
sort burned."

"So?" Lord Scuggate growled.

"So ... burn her! Tomorrow at noon in
the market square. Queen Mary will
thank you for the rest of her blood-soaked
life!"

"Perfect!" Lord Scuggate chuckled. "Tomorrow at dawn we find Old Nan."

"She could be out on the moors, collecting herbs at this time of the year," the priest reminded him.

"We'll track her down. That's what my hunting dogs are for," he said, and threw a scrap of meat to the snapping hounds on the floor.

Lord Scuggate raised his wine cup and clashed it against the raised cups of the other two.

"Here's to good Queen Mary ... and a death to all her enemies – especially Old Nan!"

Chapter Three
The Cottage in
the Heather

I cleared the tables after their lordships
had staggered to their beds. Then I crept
back down to the main hall and found
the two shaggy hounds asleep by the
guttering fire.

I fed them with plates of meat till they could eat no more. They groaned, rolled over and slept.

But I couldn't sleep. I had work to do.

I took a black woollen cloak from the stables and slipped out into the cool light of the quarter moon. Rats scuttered out of my way as I padded across the yard in my bare feet and on to the dusty road.

The church clock creaked and chimed one. Dogs barked at me but no one lit a candle or looked to see who was passing their door. At the edge of the town I turned off the road and on to the trails that led over the moor to Butterburn.

The heather was tough and tangled, but I followed the twisting sheep trails up into the hills. If I stepped on an adder I'd have died. But if I didn't go on then poor Old Nan would die.

After half an hour, I saw her tiny
cottage of tumbled stone with a roof
of heather.

Everything was silent. I didn't want
to disturb her. I sank onto the heather,
pulled the cloak over me and slept.

When the sun rose three hours later,
I woke with a start. A woman was looking
down at me. She was probably about
forty years old but the harsh life had
turned her hair grey and wrinkled her
skin dry like tree bark.

"Nan!" I said.

"Young Meg," she nodded. "Come for a cure? At this time of the morning?"

"No, I've come to warn you about Lord Scuggate," I told her.

"I remember him when he was young. An idle and vicious lad," she said, shaking her head. "His father spoiled him – oldest son, you see?" Suddenly she looked at me sharply. "What's he up to now?"

I rose stiffly to my feet. "It's a long story."

"Then come inside," she said and walked towards the cottage without looking back. "A tale is better told when you have goat's milk and oatcakes inside you ... with heather honey."

Far away, the Bewcastle church clock struck five. Hounds howled. I didn't have much time.

Chapter Four
The Lord of a
Burning Manor

When the clock struck twelve noon that day, Queen Mary rode up to the gates of Scuggate Manor. Her captain hammered on the great front gate. A kitchen boy tugged it open a crack and looked out.

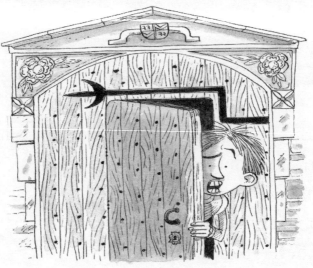

"Where is Lord Scuggate?" the angry captain growled.

The kitchen boy wiped his nose on his sleeve.

"Snnncccct! Dunno, pal! Lord Scuggate went out hunting on the moors at sunrise. He's never usually this late, though. His dinner's getting cold. He never likes to miss his dinner."

The poor people of Bewcastle had come from the fields and the houses to stare at the queen and her soldiers and servants.

Children with runny noses threw mud at the polished breastplates of her guards...

...then ran and hid behind their mothers' skirts.

The queen turned her flat, pasty face
to the captain of the guard. "What sort of
greeting is this for a queen?"

The captain shrugged. "A messenger
was sent to warn Lord Scuggate last
night, Your Majesty."

She looked at the barred gate and her
voice rose. "So? Where is Lord Scuggate?"

Along the road ran a man, dripping water. He raised clouds of dust from his boots and stumbled when the sole of one flapped and let in stones. His breeches were torn and tangled with brambles. His cap slipped down over his sweating red face and his jerkin was muddy.

"I am Lord Scuggate, Your Majesty;
sorry, Your Majesty, I was delayed."

The queen looked at him with disgust.
"Delayed?"

"I was trying to catch a witch, Your
Majesty," he whined and mopped his face
with a muddy sleeve – just wiping streaks
of brown on his purple cheeks.

"Where is this witch?" the queen demanded. She wrinkled her nose as if he stank like a tramp – which he did.

"She escaped, Your Majesty. I was planning to burn her in the market place, as a sort of welcome for Your Majesty! We people of Bewcastle know how much you enjoy a good burning!" he said, flopping his hands weakly.

The captain of the guard drew his sword and strode towards Lord Scuggate.

He smacked the lord on the back with the flat of the sword. "How dare you!" he hissed.

"Her Majesty's judges may send some evil men to be burned. But Her Majesty does not like to do it."

The captain slapped Lord Scuggate on the backside and the fat lord howled.

"Ouch! Sorry! We had heard about Bloody Mary and..."

Smack! "Never call her that! How dare you!"

Smack! "Ouch! Sorry, Queen Bloody..."

Smack! "Ouch! Sorry..."

The queen turned in her saddle and looked at Scuggate Manor.

"Is this pitiful pile yours?" she asked.

"Yes, Your Queen-ness," Lord Scuggate babbled and burbled.

"I will show you who enjoys a good burning!" She turned to her captain. "Burn down his house!"

Before the clock struck quarter past, the stables had been emptied of horses and the hay set alight. The servants fled as the fire spread. The powder in the gun-room exploded and the sky was filled with crimson flames and black smoke.

Queen Mary nodded. She turned her horse and led her followers away from Bewcastle.

A sobbing Lord Scuggate was led away to the stocks to be pelted with rotting fruit.

There is a hill that looks down on the town. A grey-haired woman in a black dress stood on the top and shook her head.

Old Nan.

Chapter Five
Sir James's
Terrible Tale

I went to the Cross Keys Inn when the
queen had gone and was given a job
as a serving maid.

I was invisible, as ever, as I served ale to
Sir James Marley and Father Walton later
that evening. I sat at a table and listened
to the tale Sir James had to tell.

"I'll never go out on those moors
again," he groaned.

Father Walton's nose, sharp as a
starling's beak, twitched. "Tell me about it."

Sir James began and I, the invisible maid, listened and smiled.

"We'd just crossed the stream at Butterburn at dawn when we saw Old Nan. She sat up on the ridge and looked towards the sunrise.

"'Hag!' we called her. 'Hag!' and 'Witch!'

"Lord Scuggate threw stones. They all missed and that just made him angrier.

'The Devil's wrapped her in his hand. We'll never hit her with a stone,' he said."

Father Walton made the sign of the cross. "The Devil can do that," he breathed.

"That's when Scuggate said we'd have to hunt her down just like a fox. He said it would make good sport. We set off through the bracken and heather.

"The sun was getting higher and it was hot work, but we didn't mind. Old Nan looked at us and hurried off over the hill. We followed her."

Father Walton nodded. "A witch can't fly her broomstick in the daylight."

"We reached the top of the hill and we could see Old Nan's cottage below us. We slipped the leashes off the dogs. The dogs leapt forwards while the witch lifted up her skirts and ran.

"She reached the battered wooden door a moment before the howling hounds. They crashed against it just as Nan threw in the bolt," Sir James said, and his eyes glowed with the memory.

"We reached the dogs and pulled them away. I called, 'Come out, Old Nan! We won't harm you!' and Scuggate hissed, 'No, *we* won't, but our dogs will tear you flesh from bone.'

"I heard her shout back through the door, 'If you don't want to harm me, leave me alone!'

"We pulled some bushes from the garden and he piled them up against the door. I took a flint from my pocket and he started up a fire."

Father Walton nodded again. "Best thing for a witch. Fire."

"The bush was dry..."

"It hasn't rained for weeks."

"Exactly, so the bush began to crackle and the gold flames took hold. Then the door began to smoulder – its ancient wood was as dry as the dust on the daisies in Old Nan's garden. The woman screamed as the door burned through.

"We stepped back to keep from being roasted alive. They saw the woman's figure, head down, burst out through the charcoal ruins of the door."

"So, you set the dogs after her? They love to hunt a running animal. They tore her into fifty pieces, I'll bet," Father Walton crooned and licked his thin lips.

"Ah, no," Sir James groaned. "That's when she used the witchcraft, isn't it?"

Chapter Six
The Flying Witch

Sir James Marley gripped his beer mug tight as he told his tale.

"Old Nan was fast as any hare. She had a start on the dogs. We lost sight of her as she ran up to the hill top. The dogs seemed too fat and full of flesh to chase her hard!"

I smiled as I listened. I'd fed those dogs well the night before.

"Then Old Nan stopped on the crest of a hill and looked back down at us. She dropped out of sight. Then the strangest thing happened. We heard a cry. 'Leave me alone!' a woman screamed. But the sound didn't come from over the hill. We looked back at the smoking ruin of Old Nan's house. And there she stood beside the doorway!"

"Witchcraft," Father Walton groaned and crossed himself again. "What did you do?"

"We lumbered back down the hill to the cottage, of course. The dogs' noses told them she was over the top of the hill. Their eyes told them she was running downhill from the house. They ran round in circles then followed us back down the hill."

"But did they catch her?"

"I'm coming to that," Sir James said and supped his ale. "The woman disappeared into a small clump of trees. When we reached it she wasn't in sight. Then we heard her cry again..."

"You had her trapped in the wood," the priest smirked.

"No! The voice came from behind us. She was at the top of the hill again! She couldn't have run! She must have flown.

We set off back up the hill and she ran.
It was a struggle but when we got to the
top ... she'd gone.

"We heard her cry, 'Leave me alone!'
and there she was – at the edge of the
wood.

"All morning we chased her. When we
thought she was in the wood, she was on
the hill top. When we thought she was on
the hill top, she was down in the wood."

"Didn't the dogs catch her?" Father Walton asked.

"I'll swear at one time they did. I saw them race up to her on the top of the hill. There was sweat in my eyes but I swear they got to her. She just stretched out a hand and patted them! They wagged their miserable tails!"

The priest moaned. "You cannot fight the Devil!"

Of course, I knew they hadn't been fighting the Devil.

I knew they had been chasing two women – Old Nan was one. I was the other. We'd made a white wig from sheep's wool for me to wear. The hunters never got close enough to see who was really on top of the hill. Nan just stayed near the wood.

Leave me alone!

We took it in turns to cry "Leave me alone!", and we watched the men run up and down the hill all the hot summer morning.

When the dogs caught me, of course they let me pat them! I was the maid that fed them!

"But that wasn't the worst," Sir James said and held his mug out for more ale. I filled it and smiled.

Chapter Seven
Old Nan's
New Guard

I knew the worst. At last
Sir James Marley of
Roughsike and Lord
Scuggate had
stumbled back
to Bewcastle
that morning.

Nan and I came together at the
smouldering ruin of her cottage.

We heard the church clock strike
a quarter to twelve and we heard his
Lordship yell, "The queen! She'll be
here soon!"

"No parade! No witch-burning!"
Sir James wailed.

Nan and I watched as the two men rushed to the bridge together and, in their panic, crashed into one another and fell into the river. It's lucky the river was low after the hot summer weather or they'd have drowned.

But they hit a pool where the town drain runs out. They came out spluttering, smelling strongly. They did not smell of sweet heather, either.

It was then that Lord Scuggate ran to meet the queen – dripping and smelling of the town toilets.

The friendly men in the local tavern laughed when I told them the story of the trick we'd played on the foul Lord Scuggate.

Next day, they climbed the hill and build a new cottage for Nan, fine enough to keep out the wicked winds that whipped Butterburn each winter.

No one helped Lord Scuggate to rebuild the manor. And he had lost all he owned in the fire. He moved in with his friend, Sir James at Roughsike. They deserve each other.

He won't be back to bother Old Nan again. And, even if he did, he'd find she has two fierce dogs to guard her. Lord Scuggate's dogs!

How did she tame the beasts? With kindness? Or with witchcraft?

Only Old Nan knows!

Afterword
Old Nan's Story

The Maid, the Witch and the Cruel Queen is a story based on real people and events in Tudor times.

Mary Tudor became queen when her brother, Edward VI, died in 1553. She was a Catholic and wanted everyone in England to worship at Catholic churches. She made a new law that said people who refused could be burned. From 1555 till she died in 1558, three hundred men and women were burned.

The people of England learned

to hate her and to call her 'Bloody Mary'. They had bonfires and parties when she died. Mary's sister, Elizabeth I, took the throne and stopped the burning of people who refused to worship in Catholic churches.

But killing 'witches' still went on.

In Tudor Britain, it was against the law to practise witchcraft. In England, the punishment was to be hanged, while in Scotland, witches were burned.

Most of the people accused of being witches were harmless old women who had no one to protect them. From 1450 to 1598 over thirty thousand people in Europe were executed as witches.

But there are some stories of women accused of witchcraft who got away with it. One of these stories was about a woman in northern England known as 'Old Nan'.

It was said that the local men tried to hunt her down, but when they chased her to the top of a hill she appeared at the bottom. No matter where they chased her she seemed to appear somewhere else calling, "Leave me alone!"

Did Old Nan use witchcraft? Or did she use a trick like the one in this story? Was there ever such a person as Old Nan? Or is she just a legend?

Only Old Nan knows!

THE ACTOR, THE REBEL AND THE WRINKLED QUEEN

Illustrated by Helen Flook

A & C BLACK

AN IMPRINT OF BLOOMSBURY

LONDON NEW DELHI NEW YORK SYDNEY

Chapter One
The Dragon
Queen

Queen Elizabeth was a monster. A
monster who had hands like claws; a red
frizzy wig like a lion's mane; a wrinkled
white face, caked with a mask of make-
up, like a corpse in a coffin; little black,
rotting teeth and
breath like
a sick old
dog.

I met her just before she died and she was the most scary thing I'd ever seen in my life.

Her dress was crusted with jewels and shone red, green, blue, orange and white, like a dragon's scaly skin. Her short, fat fingers pinched my ear and she dragged me forward so my button nose was a hand's breadth away from her hooked beak of a nose.

That's when I smelled her stinking breath and heard her creaking voice hiss to my face.

"The worst is death, and death will have its day," she breathed.

"Yes, Your Majesty," I tried to say, but my mouth was dry and I just squeaked, "Yessum-ad-stee!"

"'Yessum-ad-stee'?" she mocked. "You are supposed to be an actor, boy. You are supposed to speak clearly, aren't you?"

"Yessum-ad-stee!"

"Does Mr Shakespeare let you speak like that on stage?"

"No-hum-ad-stee!"

"Then do not speak like that to your queen!" she snarled.

At last she let me go and I swayed, almost fainting. A small, round man with a white beard grasped my arm and held me up. He was Lord Cecil, the queen's chief minister.

She turned her little dark eyes on him. "Let the boy kneel ... Dwarf."

Lord Cecil chewed his lip. I could tell he hated being called Dwarf.

"Do you want to die?" the queen asked suddenly.

"No!" I said and my voice was loud and clear this time. Lord Cecil gave me a small kick on the ankle.

"No ... Your Majesty," I said more softly,

and lowered my eyes to the cold stone
floor.

"Then you know what you must do?"
Lord Cecil asked in a kindly voice.

"Tell you the truth," I nodded.

"One lie and you go back to the prison
cell," Queen Elizabeth said. "Or we may
take you along to the Tower of London
to let you try out some of our torture

machines. The rack, the red-hot pincers, the thumbscrews..."

"I'll tell the truth!" I moaned. "I will!"

"Then let us begin," the queen commanded, and she sat back on her throne to listen.

I told my story...

Chapter Two
The Red-haired Girl

My name is James Foxton and I come from a village near York in the north of England. When I was five years old, a troupe of actors came and put on a show.

It was magical. For two hours I forgot the misery of my empty belly and the cold that bit at my bare feet.

"I want to be an actor just like them," I told my parents.

My father laughed, but my mother said, "The boy can sing and dance well enough. Let him join a company of actors. He'll be one less hungry mouth for us to feed. We haven't enough food as it is. The lad will only starve to death if we keep him at home."

So, at the age of seven, I joined Mr William Shakespeare's actors at The Globe theatre in London. At first I helped with the costumes and helped the actors to dress and made sure they had the right swords and crowns or wigs or wine bottles before they went on stage. Then I was given a small part as a fairy in Mr Shakespeare's play, *A Midsummer Night's Dream*.

Of course, all the parts were played by boys and men – girls and women were not allowed to act on the stage. That's what started the argument with the blue-eyed, red-haired girl at The Black Bull inn. We often put on a play in the yard of some inn like The Black Bull.

I was a fairy called Cobweb, and at the end the crowd cheered and clapped when I came on stage to take my bow.

The red-haired girl just glared at me from the doorway into the bar-room. When I had changed out of my dress, I went into The Black Bull to eat. The girl served greasy mutton stew and spilled it onto my shoulder.

"Oh dear, what a shame!" she smirked.

I knew she had done it on purpose.

She mopped at it with a dirty rag and I pushed her hand away.

"Ooooh! Is the little fairy girl upset?"
she asked.

"Shut up," I snapped.

"Ooooh! Will the
fairy girl change my
head into a donkey's
head, like she did in
the play?"

My fists went tight
and I jumped to my feet.
I kept my temper. "I do
not need to change your
head into a donkey's. It is ugly enough
already." I felt pleased with that.

She raised one red-brown eyebrow.
"I could act better than you," she said.
"In fact, there's a cat in the back alley
that could act better than you! You try
to skip around like a girl," she laughed,
dancing around the room clumpily. "Dad's
chickens can dance better than you."

The landlord appeared in the doorway.
"That's enough, Miranda," he said to her.
"Yes, Father," she sighed.

She walked to the door, turned for one
last look at me and poked out her tongue.

The landlord cleared his throat and called, "His Lordship, the Earl of Essex is here to see Master Shakespeare!"

There was a sudden silence in the room, then a great shuffling of chairs as the actors hurried to empty the room I stood there with my mouth open as

the tall, handsome and richly dressed
earl marched into the room, sword
clattering at his side and long beard
flowing – the old queen's favourite and
her most powerful lord.

Some people whispered she wanted to marry him and make him her king! Some whispered she was annoyed because he acted like a king already.

Suddenly, I felt my arm pulled viciously. It was the Miranda girl. She dragged me to the doorway. "It's a secret meeting, halfwit! Get out!"

But I wondered what the secret was...

Chapter Three
The Master of the Globe

The earl pulled the curtain across the
door. The passage I stood in was dark.
I stayed at the curtain and heard the
Earl of Essex talk to my master.

"William, my friend, how are you?" the earl boomed.

Mr Shakespeare said, "This is an honour!"

"It's an honour for me," the earl told him.

"That's what I meant – an honour for you!" Mr Shakespeare laughed and the earl joined the laughter.

Suddenly the girl hissed in my ear, "Spy!"

"It can't be that secret, or they wouldn't be talking so loudly," I said.

"Big ears," she sneered at me.

"Donkey ears," I spat back in the dim light.

Suddenly, we knew that the two men were talking quietly now.

We both crept back to the curtain to listen. And what we heard was the thing that almost cost me my life.

"Next Wednesday you are doing a play at The Globe theatre, aren't you, William?" the earl was asking.

"We are doing my play, *The Merchant of Venice*," my master told him.

"Hmm," the Earl of Essex said, and we heard his feet pacing the floor of the room. The girl, Miranda, snatched the knife from my belt. I almost cried out.

The footsteps stopped. Miranda used my knife to make a small slit in the curtain. She handed me back my knife, then put her eye to the hole she had made.

I copied her.

The tall earl was looking out of the window. "I want you to perform your play about King Richard the Second," he said.

Master Shakespeare shook his head slowly. "It's a long time since we did that. Some of my actors have never done it. We need more than a week to get it ready," he argued. "Next month, maybe."

The earl turned. "No it *must* be next Wednesday." He walked back to the table where my master sat. "You can do it, William."

Master Shakespeare spread his hands. "But the queen hates that play. It is a play about rebels who kill their king. She is terrified that it will give people ideas. She is scared someone will see the play and try to kill her!"

The earl took a purse from his belt and threw it on the table. "There has

been a plague all summer. The theatres
have been closed. They have just opened
again and you are desperate for money,
William."

"Yes, but…"

"There are forty shillings in cash in
that purse. Your actors can be paid again
and eat and drink in a
good tavern – not
in a rat-hole like
this place!"

Miranda went suddenly stiff and I thought she was going to cry out.

But at that moment, the earl marched towards the curtain and we stood up and tumbled down the dark corridor, out of sight, till the tall man left.

Later that evening, Master Shakespeare called the actors together. "The good news is that you can be paid at last."

The men and boys all cheered.

"The bad news is we must work night and day so we can perform *Richard II* next Wednesday."

So Master Shakespeare had taken the bribe. It was a huge and deadly mistake that would cost a man his head.

Chapter Four
Muttering Men

The next week was madder than Prince
Hamlet's granny. Every morning we were
up at dawn to practise *Richard II* and
every afternoon we acted *A Midsummer
Night's Dream* – in the middle of winter!

At night we had dinner at The Black
Bull. On the Tuesday night, Miranda
served my chicken broth without spilling
it. She hissed in my ear, "You're getting
better, fairy!"

"I have a bigger part in *Richard II*," I told her.

"I'll have to come and see you tomorrow afternoon," she said and smiled. I decided it would be the best performance of my life. I didn't know it could have been the last performance of my life.

The Globe theatre packed in two thousand people. The flag flew over the theatre to show the play was about to start.

31

I was squinting through the curtains
to see if I could see where Miranda was
standing. But at the back of the theatre,
in the shadow of the little rooms, men
were gathering and talking.

I couldn't take my eyes off them: men in
rich cloaks and swords – only a gentleman
could wear a sword; men with hard faces,
speaking from the corners of tight mouths.

They all moved up to the Earl of
Essex, had a few whispered words and
then settled to watch the play. Somehow
I knew I was watching a plot being
hatched. A plot to put the Earl of Essex
on the throne.

A cannon fired and I jumped – it was only the signal for our play to begin.

The play went well ... but when our King Richard was murdered, the gentlemen in the shadows laughed and nodded happily.

When we danced a jig at the end of the play, I leapt higher than anyone. Miranda cheered and clapped. I was happy.

Next day, the rebellion came. One day that will go down as 'history'. At the time it was a shock and a wonder ... and I was there!

Chapter Five
Terrible Treason

"Rebellion!" someone cried in the hallway of The Black Bull the next morning. We dragged on our clothes and stumbled to the door still half-asleep.

Two hundred riders clattered down
the road towards Westminster Hall.
Gentlemen with glittering swords and
fine horses; the same gentlemen who had
met at the theatre the day before. At the
head of the riders was the Earl of Essex.

"Join me, my friends!" he cried to the people on the streets. "The queen is too old to rule! It is time she went off into some quiet country palace to spend her last days in peace! Let me rule England, my dear friends. Follow me to Richmond Palace. When the queen sees you all, she will know it is time to go!"

An old man and his wife served in The Black Bull. They looked out at the earl.

"What did he say?" the old woman said and her voice trembled.

"He says he wants to be Queen!" the old man muttered.

"He can't do that!" his wife laughed. She stuck her head out into the street. "Here! Young man! You can't be Queen! We've already got one!"

Then she ducked back in before he could see who had shouted.

The crowd laughed and shuffled their feet and began to drift away.

The old woman became braver.

"Go home to your mum!" she yelled. "And put that sword away before you cut yourself!" She ducked back inside.

The earl was becoming desperate.

"You have had years of plague and years of hunger. You people of England have had to feed your children on cats and dogs and even nettle roots!"

"I'll bet it tastes better than my wife's cooking!" the old man called, joining in the fun. His wife smacked him around the head with a wet cloth.

"People of England, I beg you ... join me! Join me! Join me!" the earl roared.

"Why do you need joining?" the old woman screamed, "Are you falling apart?"

Furious horsemen raised their swords and looked towards The Black Bull.

"You'll get yourself chopped," her husband warned her.

"No, she won't," a voice behind him said. "It's the Earl of Essex who'll get himself chopped." It was Master Shakespeare ... and he was right.

The queen's troops arrived in an hour and they met the earl's little band of rebels. The people of London refused to join his revolt. The two hundred gentlemen gave up after only a short struggle.

But my struggles were just about to begin...

Chapter Six
The Cold, Grey Prison

Once the Earl of Essex had been locked in the Tower of London, the queen sent her soldiers after all the people who may have helped the revolt. People like us. Master Shakespeare and our acting troupe were dragged from our beds that night and taken to the prison at Newgate.

They gave us water. If we wanted a candle for light, wood for a fire, straw for a bed or food, then we had to pay.

I had no money. I slept on the cold stone floor and wept. The next day Miranda bought me some bread and cheese. One of the thieves who shared my cell stole it.

After three days, I was taken before Lord Cecil – the man the queen called her 'Dwarf'. As I said, I was almost fainting with fear as I faced the monster queen.

"When you acted out your play, *Richard II*, that was a signal for all the plotters to start the rebellion," Lord Cecil said.

"I know that now," I nodded.

"The question is, did Mr Shakespeare know that? Was he part of the plot?" Queen Elizabeth asked and her white make-up cracked around the eyes as she scowled at me.

"Mr Shakespeare had no idea!" I said. She jabbed a claw finger at me. "Mr Shakespeare had a meeting with the Earl of Essex a week before the play was shown. A secret meeting."

"But the earl didn't tell my master why he wanted to see that play!" I cried.

The queen gave a sour smile. "How would you know?" she hissed. "It was a secret meeting."

"I was listening at the door," I told her.

Lord Cecil looked at me sharply. "Were you? By god's nails, you are the only person who knows the truth then!"

"I do!" I nodded.

The queen snorted. "You would lie to save your precious Master Shakespeare," she said.

"But..."

"Don't argue with me," she went on fiercely. "There is only one way to make sure you are telling the truth." She turned to her little minister. "Take him to the Tower. Let the torturers work on him. Screw his thumbs till they bleed and stretch him on the rack till he's six feet tall!"

Lord Cecil bowed low and turned to one of the guards.

"Wait!" I said. "There was someone else there. A girl. The inn-keeper's daughter. She's not a friend of Master Shakespeare. She'll tell the truth!"

Lord Cecil looked at the queen. After a minute she said, "Send for her."

It took two hours for the queen's guard to find Miranda and bring her to the palace. Two hours in which I had a hideous thought. I had saved myself from torture for a little while, but maybe they would torture Miranda instead...

Chapter Seven
The Willing
Witness

Miranda came into the queen's great hall,
dropped a curtsey and looked down at
me with a frown.
I didn't dare
meet her stare.

Suddenly Queen Elizabeth rose from the throne and hobbled towards Miranda. "Don't be afraid, girl," she said and her voice was suddenly sweet.

"I'm not afraid, Your Majesty. Just curious," Miranda said pertly.

"Ah! A brave-hearted lass. I like that."

The queen did something I didn't expect. She smiled.

Lord Cecil put questions to Miranda and she answered them quickly.

"And do you think Master Shakespeare knew this was part of the plot?"

"Oh no!" Miranda smiled. "He only did it for the money – forty shillings."

Lord Cecil looked at the queen. "Shall I have the girl tortured now, Your Majesty?" he asked.

Miranda gasped. "Tortured?" She glared at me and I knew she'd never forgive me now she saw the danger I had led her into. "Why?"

But Queen Elizabeth snapped, "Don't be foolish, Dwarf! The girl is clearly a truthful child."

Lord Cecil shrugged his shoulders. "I thought the boy was truthful, but you wanted him tortured. How can you tell the girl is not a liar?" he asked.

The queen placed a wrinkled hand on Miranda's head. "Because she is just like I was when I was her age." The queen patted her frizzy, orange wig, then patted Miranda's head. "The girl has red hair, just like me! We red-haired girls are the bravest and the best people in the whole world. Isn't that so, Miranda?"

Miranda grinned. "Yes, Your Majesty."

I think my mouth must have fallen open with surprise.

The queen ordered Miranda, "Take this boy back to your tavern and look after him, child. Keep him out of trouble – keep him out of my torture rooms!" she cackled.

"I'll try, Your Majesty," Miranda promised as I blushed as red as Elizabeth's wig.

"After all," the queen sighed. "He is just a young man, and we know what men are like."

"Hopeless," Miranda said with a shake of her head. She tossed her head at me. "Well, boy? I'd better get you back to The Black Bull and start looking after you!"

I followed her to the door. I stopped a moment. I looked back. The queen and Lord Cecil were laughing.

"What is it, young man?" Queen Elizabeth asked.

"Couldn't I ... wouldn't you...?"

"What?"

"Wouldn't you ... rather send me back to prison?" I groaned.

I felt a sharp tug on my sleeve as I was dragged away from a red-haired queen by a red-haired girl.

Afterword
The Essex
Rebellion

The Actor, the Rebel and the Wrinkled Queen is a story based on real people and events in Tudor times.

The Earl of Essex was a wild young man but old Queen Elizabeth was very fond of him. She called him her 'Wild Horse'.

The earl was known as the 'most popular man in England'. As Elizabeth grew old and feeble he decided to see if he was popular enough to be chosen as the ruler of England.

First, he had to capture Elizabeth. He gathered the two hundred plotters together and rode into London on 8 February 1601. He had made a huge mistake. The people of London were poor and hungry and unhappy with the queen's rule. But they weren't traitors. They refused to join Essex. He was arrested without much of a fight.

On 25 February he was beheaded.

The play, *Richard II*, was performed as a signal for the rebellion to begin. Queen Elizabeth was furious that William Shakespeare had acted the play at The Globe theatre and she had him arrested with his actors. The question was, did Shakespeare know the show was part of a plot? Or did he just perform it for the money? In time, the queen released Shakespeare – she seemed to believe he was not to blame.

But was he? What is the truth? What happened when the Earl of Essex met Shakespeare to ask him to perform? We will never know.

Elizabeth did give Shakespeare and the actors a small punishment for their crime. She said they had to perform a play for her free of charge. Shakespeare agreed. The queen wanted to know she was not afraid of plots. So what play did she make them perform?

Richard II ... of course!

TERRY DEARY'S TALES